AN UNOFFICIAL **ROBLOX** BOOK

DIARY OF A
ROBLOX
PRO

DRAGON
PET

By Ari Avatar

First published by Scholastic Australia Pty Limited in 2022.
This edition published by Scholastic in the UK, 2023
1 London Bridge, London, SE1 9BG
Scholastic Ireland, 89E Lagan Road, Dublin Industrial Estate,
Glasnevin, Dublin, D11 HP5F

ISBN 978 0702 32933 3

A CIP catalogue record for this book is available from the British
Library.

Printed in the UK by CPI Group UK (Ltd), Croydon, CR0 4YY
Paper made from wood grown in sustainable forests and other
controlled sources.

1 3 5 7 9 10 8 6 4 2

www.scholastic.co.uk

MONDAY LUNCHTIME

DING, DING, DING!

Phew! I was so happy to hear the lunch bell ring. Mr. Brickhouse had been going on and on and ON in our History lesson and I was **SO BORED.** We were learning about ancient civilizations and how they used the invention of the block to create world landmarks. I was sure Mr. Brickhouse was going to call my name to answer a question, which would have been a disaster because I hadn't been listening.

Talk about being saved by the lunch bell!

I walked out of History class and headed to my locker. I dumped my books inside and pulled out my lunch bag. But as I turned to leave, I **SMACKED** right into somebody. The crash was so hard I went flying backward and landed straight onto my butt. I even slid down the corridor a little and made a squeaky stopping sound.

OOF!

"Watch it, **BLOCKHEAD!**" an angry voice sneered.

I didn't even have to look up to see who it was. Trip. The school bully who also happened to be the mayor's son.

He thought he was the biggest pro around and got away with everything just because his mom is the mayor. But I knew the truth about Trip. He wasn't a pro at all. He was the biggest **SCAREDY-AVATAR** in the world. And he was a total fake. I knew all his stories about being cool and brave were made up.

"You knocked *me* over!" I said angrily.

Trip's block face softened slightly. He put out his hand to help me up.

Weird.

I cautiously took his hand as he pulled me to my feet, but as I was almost standing, Trip suddenly let go, sending me **CRASHING** back down. Hard.

OOF!

"Psych!" Trip cackled.

His blockhead friends, Elle and Levi, joined in as they walked off down the hall.

LAME.

I stood up, rubbed my sore butt, and walked outside to find my friends.

"Ari, over here!" Jez waved to me from the grassy area next to the courtyard.

It was a warm, sunny day, so we liked to sit under the tree for some shade.

"What's up?" my other best friend, Zeke, said when

he saw the frown on my wide face.

"Just Trip being a pain again," I told them.

"Ignore him," Jez said, rolling her eyes.

I sat down and unzipped my lunch bag. Inside was a sandwich my dad had made for me. I took a bite. Not bad.

NOM, NOM, NOM.

"So, what's up with you avatars?" I said in between mouthfuls of food.

"Well," Jez said, her wide face

brightening, "last night I **HACKED** into another army account—"

"I'm not listening!" Zeke interrupted, covering his ears. His dad is in the army and he didn't want to know about Jez's illegal activity.

Jez ignored Zeke. "I think I've found where there might be another **PORTAL.**"

Jez is a computer whiz. She is an amazing hacker, but her life dream was to find a portal. Portals were really rare—some avatars didn't even believe they existed. But she was totally sure they did and she was obsessed with discovering one.

"What about you, Zeke?" I said.

"I think my **EGG** is going to hatch today!" he said, looking excited.

"Whoa, no way!" I said. "Any idea what animal you've got?"

Zeke shook his head. "Nah, but I think it's **SUPER RARE.**"

"How come?" Jez asked.

"It has a really cool pattern on the shell. I've never seen anything like it," Zeke said. "Hey, why don't you both come to my place after school and you can see it? You might even get to watch it hatch!"

Jez and I looked at each other. "Yeah, cool!" we both said at once.

I wanted to see Zeke's egg, but I also wanted an excuse to go to his house. Zeke has the **COOLEST** house of any avatar I know. That's because his dad is an obby designer for the army. He was always creating samples and prototypes in their backyard to test before making the real thing. That's why Zeke is such a pro at obbys. He is a **PARKOUR PRO** too, and can do the coolest jumps and stunts.

"Which pet do you want the most?" Jez asked.

Zeke thought for a moment. "Any pet would be awesome. I've never had one before."

"Yeah, but what's your **DREAM PET?**" Jez said.

"My dream pet? Um . . . I dunno . . .
maybe a dog? Like yours, Ari!"

My dog was always happy to see
me, with her little tail wagging
CRAZILY back and forth. It
was like she had a smile on her
face all the time. But she wasn't
rare. I'd heard one avatar at
school had hatched a giraffe!
Now that would be cool.

"Coda?" I said. "Yeah, she's cute, but
she's not, like, super rare or anything."

The bell pierced through the air
and made us all jump.

"Better go—I've got Ms. Markson for Math," Zeke said. He launched his body up from his seated position into a squat. Then he jumped into the air and did a backward somersault to stand up.

"Show-off," I teased.

"Meet you avatars at the front gate this afternoon to go to my house!" Zeke said as he jogged off to class.

"Can't wait!" I yelled after him.

MONDAY AFTER SCHOOL

Zeke, Jez, and I walked back to Zeke's house, which was only a short distance from school. We strolled up the long driveway, which was crazy long and steep—perfect for parkour and **SKATING STUNTS!** Although, there was that one time I tried a kickflip on my skateboard while traveling at what felt like a hundred miles per hour. I still had the scar to prove it.

We ran up to his front door and Zeke let us in.

"I'm home!" Zeke yelled up the stairs.

We wandered into the kitchen and dumped our bags on the floor.

"Hungry?" Zeke asked.

"Starving," said Jez. I nodded in agreement.

Zeke grabbed juice from the fridge and chips from the pantry.

"Are you eating a healthy snack?"

Zeke's dad's voice floated down the stairwell.

We glanced at one another.

"Uh, yeah!" Zeke yelled back.

Jez and I laughed.

"What? Potato chips—they're practically vegetables. And juice is fruit, right?" Zeke said, shrugging.

"Yeah, right," I said.

"So, where's the egg?" Jez asked as she grabbed a handful of chips.

"Outside. Dad made a little
nest for it with a warming light
and everything."

Zeke's dad was so good at making
things. He mostly made obbys but
could do other stuff too.

"Can we see?" I asked.

Zeke nodded and gestured for us
to follow him out the back door.
We exited to the backyard, where
there was a hutch that probably
had the egg in it. But I was way
too **DISTRACTED** by what
else I saw.

"Whoa, bruh!" I exclaimed.

"Oh yeah, that's a new demo obby my dad is building for the army," Zeke said.

Jez and I looked at each other with wide eyes. It was **SO COOL!** There was a wall with a steep slope that you had to run up to get to the top. Then there were **FLOATING BLOCKS** that you had to jump onto, like stepping stones across a river. I had no idea how Zeke's dad made them float in midair, but they looked **SICK!**

"What goes under the floating blocks?" I asked, pointing.

"Well, on this demo model, nothing. But IRL, it would probably be raging floodwaters or even lava."

"AWESOME!" Jez and I breathed.

"And that's not all," a voice said
from behind us. It was Zeke's
dad. He had the same wide head
and dark hair as his son. "Check
this out," he said, walking over
to the obby.

He hit a button on the side of one
of the panels and out from the
ground shot up a row of sharp
wooden spikes.

"Whoa!" we all yelled.

"Man, I wouldn't want to be the

avatar who fell onto those. **OOF!"**
I said.

"Well, we have to train for these life-and-death situations, you know," Zeke's dad answered.

Suddenly, we heard a
RUSTLING SOUND
coming from behind us.

"Hey, is that your egg, Zeke?" his dad asked.

We all ran over to the hutch, which was shaking lightly.

Zeke gently lifted the lid and we peered in. His egg was **AWESOME.** It was a candy-pink color with stripes all over it. It began to wobble from side to side, like it was going to **BREAK OPEN.**

"It's totally hatching!" Jez yelled.

We held our breath.

The egg cracked slightly—a small zigzag line appearing across the middle.

"Come on, little guy," Zeke coaxed.

It continued to shake and more cracks appeared all over the egg. A tiny hole opened up and we saw something long and sharp peek out of the top.

"Is that a claw?" Zeke's dad said. "I hope it's not one of those tigers the neighbors got."

It cracked more until it finally wobbled and fell on its side. The top of the egg was kicked off, revealing Zeke's new pet.

"He's so **CUTE!**" Jez yelled as two enormous brown eyes looked up at us.

The hair on the pet began to dry and it stretched out its long arms.

"It's a **SLOTH!**" I said excitedly. "You're so lucky—they're **SUPER RARE!** And I've heard you can teach them awesome things like dance moves."

"**WOW!**" Zeke said, picking up his new baby pet.

"What are you going to call him?" Zeke's dad said.

Zeke thought for a minute. "I think I'll call him **DASH.**"

"Dash?" said Jez. "You do know sloths are, like, the slowest animals ever."

"I'm being ironic!" Zeke smirked. "Besides, I think he likes it. Dash?"

The sloth looked up at Zeke with his huge brown eyes. He stretched out his long arms and yawned, then fell asleep in Zeke's arms.

"I wish I had a **COOL PET,**" I said, stroking Dash's head.

"Um, what about Coda?" Jez said.

Sure, my dog was loyal and playful, and she could be heaps of fun, but she wasn't as interesting as a sloth. I mean, how many avatars actually owned a sloth?

"Yeah, she's good . . ." I mumbled. "But she's **A LOT** of work. I have to feed her and walk her and . . ." I trailed off.

"I don't have any pets," Jez said.

"My mom is allergic. Maybe you should be happy with what you have."

I wrinkled my nose. I didn't like being schooled by my friend.

"Should we try the obby?" I said, to change the subject.

"If it's OK with you avatars, I might just hang out with Dash for a while," Zeke said.

"Yeah, no probs. I've gotta go anyhow," Jez said.

"Me too. I've got boring chores
to get through, otherwise I don't
get my screen time. **LAME!**"
I grumbled.

"See you at school tomorrow!"
Zeke said.

As he walked us back to the door,
I looked at Dash. He was SO cool. I
couldn't help feeling a little jealous.

MONDAY NIGHT

At dinner, I couldn't stop talking about Dash the Sloth.

"And he has the **LONGEST ARMS!** Zeke said he's going to train him to do obbys with him. How amazing is that?"

"Yeah, yeah, we get it," my sister, Ally, said, rolling her eyes.

"What's your **PROBLEM?**" I said, annoyed.

"You've been going on and on about Zeke's pet. It's getting kinda boring," she said.

RUDE.

"Yeah, well, if I had a pet as unusual as Dash, I'd be outside training him right now!" I said.

I heard a whimper at my feet. I looked down and my dog, Coda, was staring up at me with begging eyes. I ignored her.

"You don't even look after the pet you've got," said Mom. "Have you fed Coda tonight? She looks **HUNGRY.**"

"I'll feed her after dinner," I dismissed. "And anyway, Coda isn't like Dash."

"That's mean," said Ally, calling Coda over and feeding her a bit of meat from her plate.

"Don't feed the dog at the table," Dad said. "And Ally's right—what's wrong with Coda?"

"Nothing is wrong with Coda," I said, rolling my eyes. "I just mean I'd like a dream pet."

"I thought Coda *was* your dream pet," Mom said.

"Nah, like a **RARE DREAM PET.** You don't understand," I said, shaking my head in frustration. I picked up my empty plate and took it over to the sink.

"FEED CODA!" Dad reminded me.

"Oh man, I'm meant to be bloxxing some noobs with Zeke right now!" I complained.

"Not until you've fed Coda,"
Mom said.

UGH.

"I'll feed her," Ally interrupted. "Yes,
I will!" she said in a baby voice,
ruffling Coda's fur.

"Ally's doing it!" I yelled as I ran
upstairs to log online to the game
Zeke and I started two days
ago. When I got there, I saw
a **MESSAGE** blinking on
the screen.

Zeke: Sorry, AFK. Dash needs me. GTG!

I facepalmed. Why did he have to be away from his keyboard now? I flopped on my bed and folded my arms.

BORING.

ZZZZZZZZZZZZZZZZZZZZ.

Nothing to do. Wish I were training a **ПЕШ** pet.

TUESDAY
MORNING

"Good morning, sleepy blockhead!"
Mom said as I trudged into
the kitchen.

"MPHRPMPH," I mumbled back,
rubbing my half-closed eyes.

Dad and Ally were already
eating breakfast and Mom was
WHIZZING up a concoction
in the blender. I walked to the
pantry and grabbed some cereal,
then I carried it over to the table,

where a bowl, spoon, and milk
were waiting.

"Sleep well?" Dad asked.

"MPHRPMPH," I mumbled.

"Ari," Mom said, sitting down next
to me, "your dad and I were
talking last night and we think we
have a **PLAN** that you might like."

I looked up.

"You know how you were saying
that you really want that—what
do you call it—dream pet?" Dad

said as he made quote marks with his fingers in the air.

"A dream pet, **YES!**" I suddenly felt wide-awake.

"Well, we think that if you can show us how responsible you are with Coda, then we might consider another pet for the family," Mom said.

I jumped up. **"YES!** I will, I promise. I'll be the best pet owner with Coda and then I'll take **SUCH** good care of my new pet! Can we get one today?"

"Hold your horses," Dad said, gesturing for me to sit down. "We want to see you looking after Coda every day. For at least a week. We want you feeding her, walking her, taking her out for bathroom breaks, and maybe even training her a bit."

As Dad said that, Coda jumped up on the side of the table and stole the end of Ally's toast.

"Hey!" she protested.

I smothered a laugh. But then I saw Dad's **SERIOUS FACE.**

"Yes, I can do that," I said. "I'll train her to be a good dog and I'll walk her and wash her and feed her and everything! Then can we go to the pet nursery and get an egg?"

"We'll reevaluate in one week," Mom said, half smiling.

AWESOME!

I devoured my breakfast and then jumped up to go get dressed for school.

"Ahem," Dad said, not so subtly.

I looked at him and he nodded his head toward Coda, who was whimpering at his feet.

"Oh yeah, right, of course!" I said, remembering my new responsibilities. "Come on, Coda!"

Coda **BOUNDED** after me as I took her to get her breakfast. After she hoovered that up, I took her outside to do her business. While we were in the backyard, she ran around in circles happily. I saw a ball on the ground, which I picked up and threw to her. She ran after it.

"OK, COME BACK!" I sang.

But she didn't.

"Coda?"

She looked up.

"Come!"

She ignored me.

Hmm. I ran back inside and got some of her tiny training treats.

"Coda, come!"

Coda came running up to me with the ball. "Now, drop it," I said.

She dropped the ball and sat, waiting for her treat.

"Good girl!" I said, ruffling her head.

I threw the ball again. "Fetch!"

When she saw I still had the treats, she came back when I called her and dropped the ball.

YES!

The next time I tried it, I didn't give her a treat.

"Coda, drop it!"

She did.

"Good dog!" I smiled at her and she wagged her little tail.

"I've gotta go to school, but we can play again this afternoon," I said, throwing her the ball one last time.

This was awesome. All I had to do was look after Coda and I'd soon have my very own dream pet. **EZ!**

TUESDAY AFTERNOON

"Look—he's pulling himself up already!" Zeke said like a proud parent.

Dash the Sloth was holding on to one of the ropes on the demo obby course and **SWINGING** lightly. He looked at the next rope, slowly swung forward, then reached out and grabbed it.

"All right!" I said as Dash made it to the next rope. "He's a natural!"

"WOOF!" Coda yapped beside me and I shushed her.

"I think Coda wants a go on the obby too." Zeke laughed.

Coda pulled forward on her leash, trying to get closer to Dash and the obby course.

"She can't do it—she's a dog," I said.

Coda whimpered.

"When I get my new pet, it'll be something so rare and cool and it'll be an obby **PRO!**" I said.

Zeke laughed again. "When do you think you'll get it?"

"I'm doing everything my parents said I have to do. I fed Coda this morning and taught her how to fetch. Then this afternoon, I've walked her here to your house and then I'll play with her at the park before I go home and give her dinner," I said, patting her head.

"EZ!" Zeke said, high-fiving me.

As I high-fived Zeke, I accidentally let go of Coda's leash. She bounded over to the obby and jumped up and grabbed the rope with her teeth. She dangled there for a moment, then **SWUNG** herself up onto the platform above.

"Whoa!" Zeke said. "Maybe Coda could be an **OBBY DOG!**"

I laughed and pulled Coda down. "I doubt it," I said. "But you wait till I get my dream pet. It'll be the biggest obby pro you have ever

seen. I'm going to train it to be a
LEGEND!"

I glanced at the clock in Zeke's
house and realized I needed to get
a move on so I could play with Coda
in the park before going home.

"Gotta go, bruh!" I said.

"Later," Zeke said as he waved
goodbye.

"Let's go, Coda!" Coda chased
after me as we ran up the side of
Zeke's house and down the road
to the park.

SATURDAY MORNING

"OK, check this out," I said.

Ally and my parents smiled as they watched me with Coda.

"Ready, girl?" I said.

Coda wagged her tail and smiled up at me.

"FETCH!" I yelled, throwing the ball across the yard.

Coda leaped up and ran across the backyard and retrieved the ball. She came back to me and dropped it at my feet, waiting expectantly for me to throw it again.

"Good girl!" I said. "Now, shake!"

Coda reached out her paw and placed it in my hand. I shook her paw and smiled at her.

"Now, dance, Coda!"

Coda jumped up on her hind legs and hopped around.

"Wow!" Ally yelled.

Mom and Dad clapped.

Coda and I **BEAMED.**

"You sure have done a good job training her," Dad said.

"And I've been taking great care of her," I added. "I've fed her every day, I've been walking her, and look how clean she is! I gave her a bath last night."

Coda **SPARKLED.**

Dad gave Mom a little look, and
Mom smiled and nodded.

"OK, Ari, I know it's been less
than a week, but your mom and I
are so impressed with how you've
trained Coda that we looked
at when the next Nursery Egg
Adoption Day is. And it turns out,
there's one this weekend," Dad said.

My eyes lit up. Could it be?

"We're happy for you to go and
choose an egg today," Mom said.

AWESOME!

"Thanks, Mom and Dad!" I yelled, high-fiving Dad. "Can we go now?!"

"Oh, I guess . . ."

"YES!"

I ran inside and up the stairs to get my shoes. Coda bounded after me.

"Sorry, girl. No walk today. I'm going to get a **NEW EGG!**"

Coda's face fell.

I bolted back down the stairs.

"Let's **GO!**" I called out.

"OK, OK, keep your blocks on," Dad mumbled as he gathered his car keys.

The drive out to the egg nursery was a long one. While we drove, I used Dad's phone to research all the different types of eggs that might be available.

"I want a really **RARE** one," I said breathlessly.

"Why?" Dad asked.

"I dunno. I just think it'd be cool to have a **DIFFERENT** kind of pet. Like Zeke's sloth."

We kept driving for what felt like forever. I couldn't stop bouncing around in my seat with excitement.

Finally, we made it to the egg nursery on the outskirts of town. It was a small, shedlike building and I could already see there were other avatars there looking for their future pets.

"Hurry up, Dad! We don't want

to miss out on the best eggs," I said impatiently as Dad parked the car.

We walked into the shed and saw rows and rows of eggs sitting in warm little nests. They were an array of colors and patterns, from pink to gold, spotty to stripy. I looked around the room with wide eyes. How was I going to choose?

A sales-avatar walked up to me. He wore a badge with the egg nursery logo on it. "What are you looking for, young avatar?"

"I want something different. I don't want something common, like a dog or a cat. Something **NOBODY** has!" I said.

He tapped his chin in thought. "I know I have some turtles over here," he said, pointing. "And while I can't be a hundred percent sure, I think this green one over here is a **MONKEY.**"

A monkey would be great. It could do the obby courses with me. But I knew three other avatars at school with monkeys.

"Yeah, maybe . . ." I said, unsure.

The sales-avatar gave me a wry smile. "I do have one very different egg," he said carefully.

My eyes lit up.

"But it's only for a very special owner who can take care of a very . . . **UNIQUE PET.**"

"I can do it! I can!" I said, jumping up and down.

He gestured for me to follow him right to the back of the shed. He took me behind the counter and pulled out a box. It was a big wooden box with a gold lock on it. After fumbling around in his pocket, he pulled out a long brass key, placed it in the lock, and turned it. The lock clunked open. When he lifted the lid, a golden light shone out of the box, turning his face a warm shade of yellow.

"What is it?" I said, trying to see.

He turned the box to face me and I gazed inside.

"WHOA!"

There was a nest of straw and on top was the most incredible egg I had  ever seen. The surface of the egg was textured and rough, with a pattern that resembled crocodile skin. But instead of being green like a croc, it **SHIMMERED GOLDEN.**

"Can I touch it?" I asked nervously.

The sales-avatar nodded.

I reached out my hand, but when I made contact with the egg, I pulled it back sharply. I wasn't expecting it to be **HOT!** It wasn't hot enough to burn, so I reached out again, gently touching it with my fingertips. The shell was rough as I felt its scales.

"Is it a crocodile?" I asked.

The sales-avatar shook his head. "I can't be sure what it is, but it's not a croc. I think it's something more . . . **SPECIAL.**"

At that moment, Dad came up behind me.

"Wow, what's that, champ?" he asked.

"It's a rare egg and I totally want it!" I said.

"It looks a bit . . . uh . . . exotic," he said, uncertain. "It's not a dinosaur, is it?" he asked.

The sales-avatar shrugged slightly.

"We never quite know. But I don't think it's a dinosaur. All I know is that this egg is very special and **VERY RARE.** Whatever is inside is going to need a lot of care and attention."

"We'll take it!" I yelled.

"Are you sure, Ari?" Dad said.

I nodded my head vigorously.

"OK, then, this is it!" Dad said.

WOO HOO!

SATURDAY AFTERNOON

Ari: Zeke, you won't believe the egg I got.

Zeke: What is it?

Ari: I dunno, but it's something EPIC.

Zeke: When will it hatch?

Ari: The avatar in the nursery thinks any day now.

> **Zeke:** COOL!

> **Ari:** GTG. Need to check the egg.

I logged off and went across my room to where I was keeping my egg. I opened the lid and the egg **GLOWED** golden.

"You are going to be the coolest pet," I told it.

The egg seemed to wiggle just a bit.

Coda **WHINED** at my feet.

"Sorry, girl, I can't walk you now. I've got an egg to take care of."

Coda whimpered and left my room as I turned my attention back to the egg. I reached out to touch it.

OUCH!

It was even hotter than this morning. I was told the egg would increase in temperature as it got ready to hatch. I put my burned finger in my mouth to soothe the pain. Whatever was in there, it was something **TOTALLY WICKED.**

MONDAY MORNING

"So, has it hatched yet?" Jez asked as we sat on the bus to school.

"Nope, but I think it'll be any day now. I can't even touch the egg without oven mitts!"

"How's Dash?" Jez asked Zeke.

"He's cool. I mean, he's kinda . . . I dunno, slow?" Zeke said.

Jez laughed. "Bruh, you know that

sloths are literally meant to be the definition of slow?"

Zeke shrugged. "I thought with his long arms he might be a bit better on the obby. But he can't do it fast enough. Not like Coda the other day."

CODA! Oh man, I forgot to feed her this morning. I was so busy checking my egg. I'd have to call Mom when I got to school to ask her to feed my dog.

"Why don't you both come over to my place after school and see the egg? It's wicked! And I think it might hatch this afternoon. Dad is keeping an eye on it today," I said.

"Sounds awesome," Zeke said.

"I'm in!" Jez said.

The bus chugged through Blockville until it pulled up outside our school.

"Ugh, I so don't feel like school today," Zeke said. "I've got History of Blocks this morning."

"I've got Economics," I said.

"I've got Coding! Woo hoo!"

We rolled our eyes at Jez.
TOTAL CODING GEEK.

We jumped off the bus and jogged through the open school gates. The bell was about to ring and we had to get our stuff ready for class.

"See you at lunch. And don't forget this afternoon at my place!" I yelled after Zeke and Jez as they disappeared down the corridor.

MONDAY AFTERNOON

Jez, Zeke, and I ran in through the front door of my house and dumped our schoolbags on the floor. I could see Mom at the dining table, which was covered in decorations for a wedding she was planning for a client. Mom's a party planner and does weddings, parties, and big events, which meant our house was often flooded with party bags and balloons and decorations. All over the table were curling vines with green leaves.

"What's with the jungle?" I teased her.

"It's the centerpiece for the wedding tables," she said, a little annoyed. "It's a forest-themed wedding, which is meant to look like *A Midsummer Block's Dream.*"

HUH?

"Oh, forget it," she said, shaking her head. "Are you avatars hungry?"

"We'll grab something in a minute," I said. "We want to go check on the egg."

Jez and Zeke waved to my mom,
then followed me upstairs.

We entered my room and ran over
to the wooden box. It had small
curls of **SMOKE** coming out of it.

"What the . . . ?" Zeke began.

I put on the oven mitts and
opened the box. A small puff of
smoke came out as soon as I
pulled off the lid. I coughed lightly.
When the smoke cleared, we
could see the egg, which was now
glowing a **GOLDEN-RED
COLOR.**

"Whoa!" Jez breathed.

"It's moving!" Zeke said excitedly.

The egg was jittering from
side to side. Was my pet
HATCHING?

"Bruh, I think you're about to meet
your pet," Zeke said.

I held my breath.

The egg skittered around the box,
falling to its side and spinning
around. There was a **TAPPING**
sound coming from the inside.

Suddenly, a large crack appeared at the top of the egg. Then, a small **BLACK CLAW** poked out.

"What on earth is in there?" Jez said.

Maybe it was a dinosaur, after all? Nervous swirls began to churn in my belly.

The egg continued to vibrate in the box, and the crack extended from the top all the way down the side. The animal within kept tapping away on the shell, trying its best to break free.

Tiny puffs of smoke came out of the cracks.

"Is it a phoenix?" Jez asked.

A thin **FLAME** burst out of the top of the egg and the shell **CRACKED** wide apart.

"I think it's a lizard," Zeke said, observing the little creature's scales.

The creature unfurled itself and sat up. It had miniature horns on its red head and **SCALES** all over its body. It also had a long tail like a crocodile.

"Is it a red croc?" Jez asked.

The creature then stretched out its tiny arms. But we all gasped as we saw what was coming out of its back. Big, black, leathery wings uncurled from its body. It extended them and flapped them lightly, which lifted its little body off the ground. It stopped flapping and fell back down with a bump.

The creature rubbed its nose, then took in three quick breaths.

"AH . . . AH . . . AH . . .

The pet sneezed and a thin stream of fire burst out of its nostrils, lightly charring the side of the box.

"Whoa, Ari. That's no croc," Jez said with wide eyes. "That's . . . that's a . . ."

I finished her sentence. "It's a **DRAGON.**"

MONDAY AFTERNOON— A BIT LATER

"A DRAGON?!" Mom squealed.

I knew she'd overreact!

"It's fine!" I protested.

"How big is this thing gonna get?" Dad said.

"I don't know, but I'll train him. He'll be fine!"

Jez and Zeke exchanged glances.

"I don't know about this, Ari,"
Mom said.

"It's fine! It's the *coolest* pet
EVER! I don't know anyone
with a dragon, right?" I said,
turning toward my friends.

Zeke and Jez nodded, but they
still looked worried.

"We'll have to think about this,"
Dad said. "For now, take him
outside. I don't want him flying
around in here."

"He can barely hover off the ground," I said. "He's **FINE.**"

Jez, Zeke, and I headed into the backyard.

"A dragon. I can't believe it," Jez said.

I looked in the box and the little red dragon smiled up at me. I gently reached in, careful to check that he didn't bite. He let me pick him up under the arms and place him on the grass.

"He's so cute!" Zeke said.

"What are you gonna call him?"
Jez asked.

I looked at the dragon.

"How about . . . Firey?"

The dragon scrunched up his face.

"OK, Scaley?"

The dragon coughed and spluttered.

"OK, not that, then. Hmm. How
about . . ." I thought as I stared
at him. His red skin seemed to
glow like . . . like an ember in the

campfire. **"EMBER?"**

The dragon hovered off the ground slightly and **CLAPPED** his wings.

"I think he likes it," Jez said.

"Ember it is, then!" I smiled.

"How are you gonna take care of a dragon?" Zeke asked, staring at Ember.

"He's only a little guy," I said, picking him up.

"But will he grow?" Jez asked.

I shrugged. I'd never seen a dragon before.

"Let's teach him some tricks," I said.

I ran inside and grabbed some of Coda's training treats. When I got back outside, I noticed Ember was **HOVERING** higher off the ground. Flying like a pro already!

"Ember, come!" I beckoned him over with the treat. He hovered in the air, then flew to me.

"Good boy!" I yelled, giving him a treat.

Ember took it, then scrunched up his nose and **SPAT** it out.

"Not a fan of dog treats, then," I said.

"What do dragons eat?" Zeke asked.

"I'll have to research it," I said. What *did* dragons eat?!

Ember hovered a little higher. He was flying above my head now.

"Uh, not too high, Ember," I said nervously.

"Maybe we should take him inside," Zeke said. "You don't want him **FLYING OFF.**"

"Good idea," I said. I picked up Ember and carried him into the house.

"Where's Mom?" I asked Dad.

"She's gone out to get some more supplies for that wedding party she's planning. I'll be upstairs with Ally doing her Science assignment. Keep that dragon under control," he said.

I nodded and Ember gave Dad a

completely innocent look. Dad shook his head and went upstairs.

I checked the pantry for something we could all eat. "We've got nothing good," I complained.

I pulled out a few things, but there wasn't anything yummy. Ember flew to us and hovered over some of the ingredients I'd put on the bench while I kept looking for more food. He made a **SQUEAKING** noise over one of the packets.

"I think he wants what's in that bag," Zeke said.

"Corn kernels?" I said, looking at Ember.

He panted with excitement.

I shrugged and poured a few kernels into a metal mixing bowl. I put it in front of Ember and he sniffed them. Then he moved back slightly.

"I thought he wanted them," Jez said, shaking her head.

Suddenly, Ember blew out a stream of fire from his nostrils. The corn kernels caught fire and

began **POPPING** in the metal bowl.
It began overflowing with . . .

"POPCORN!"

"Clever boy!"
I exclaimed.

Ember shared the
popcorn with Zeke, Jez, and me.

"How unreal is your pet? He's a
popcorn machine!" Jez laughed.

As we munched on the popcorn,
Ember explored the room. He
flew **HIGHER** and with more

confidence. Soon he was touching the ceiling.

"Not *too* high, Ember," I warned.

He gained speed as he became more confident using his wings. Soon he was flying around the room **REALLY FAST,** dodging from left to right.

"Um, Ari," Jez said.

"Slow down, Ember," I called.

He kept zooming around, **KNOCKING** into things as

he went. A vase of flowers tipped over, splashing water onto the floor.

"Ember, stop!" I yelled.

He didn't.

He **BUMPED** into the cupboards and knocked over a bag of rice, which sent grains spilling all over the floor.

He then knocked over the clock on the wall, which **CRASHED** down with a bang.

"What's going on?" I heard Dad ask from upstairs.

"Ember, STOP!" we all yelled in unison.

But he continued flying around the kitchen, causing **CHAOS!**

"STOP!" I screamed.

Ember did stop for a moment. Maybe he was starting to obey?

As he hovered, he breathed in three quick breaths.

"AH . . . AH . . . AH . . . CHOOOOOO!"

Flames shot out of his nostrils, flying across the room and toward the dining table. They engulfed the green ivy that sat on the table for Mom's wedding decorations.

"NOOOOO!"

But it was too late. The leaves were **ON FIRE.**

Zeke grabbed the vase that held the remaining water from when it tipped over. He chucked it at the ivy and the blaze went out. But the leaves were a black smoldering mess.

OOF.

I ran over to Coda and pulled off her collar. I grabbed Ember and snapped the collar around his neck. Then I grabbed Coda's leash and attached it to Ember so he couldn't fly away from me.

"What on **EARTH** is going on in here?!" Mom cried.

I glanced around the room at the mess that Ember had caused. It looked like there'd been an explosion.

"ARI!!!!!!!" Mom yelled.

TUESDAY MORNING

BEEP! BEEP!

My alarm woke me from my deep sleep. I rolled over sleepily, smacking the snooze button. I opened one eye and then jumped up with fright.

"AAAAGH!"

I'd put Ember in a dog crate that used to belong to Coda. He'd fit really nicely in there last night and I thought it would be like a cozy cave for him. But this morning, he was **FIVE TIMES** the size of yesterday and was bursting through the bars.

"Ember! What happened?!" I exclaimed.

I opened the crate door and Ember rolled out. He stretched his wings, which knocked the lamp off my desk. His wings ripped the posters off my wall, and when he shot upward he crashed into the ceiling. He let out a yelp, but not as loud as my own yelp when I realized he'd dented the ceiling.

"Oh man!"

I took him by the hand and led him down the stairs. He was as big as I was! As he walked with me, his wings knocked the photos off the wall. I winced at every **CRASH** he made, knowing Mom and Dad were not going to be OK with this.

And **SPOILER ALERT:**
they were not OK with this.

"If he's grown this much overnight,
imagine how **HUGE** he will be in
a week!" Mom argued.

"He might just be having a quick
growth spurt," I said desperately.
"Please don't get rid of him!"

"What are we going to do with
him?" Dad said.

"We can put him outside for today.
I'll get a really long leash and
he can play in the backyard, but

with the leash he won't fly away. **PLEASE?"** I begged.

Mom and Dad exchanged concerned glances.

"OK for now," Dad said. "But we are really going to have to rethink this arrangement."

"You'd better get ready," Mom said, looking at her watch. "It's the Sports Fun Day today and you don't want to miss out."

EPIC! I'd forgotten it was the **SPORTS FUN DAY.**

It was one of the best days of the year. We got to miss school for a whole day and do races as well as fun outdoor games. There were also yummy food stalls where we could get things like sausages for lunch and snow cones for dessert. **NOM, NOM, NOM!**

Dad helped me find a long chain in the garage and I attached it to Ember. Then I tied it to a big, strong tree trunk.

Ember whimpered.

"It's OK, boy," I said, patting his

snout. "I'll be home this afternoon. And if you're good, I'll let you have more popcorn!"

Ember's eyes lit up at the word "popcorn."

I gave him a pat goodbye and raced out to the bus. It was going to be an **AWESOME** day!

TUESDAY LUNCHTIME

The Sports Fun Day was
AMAZING!

Zeke won all his races because
he's a **PRO.** He was extra
fast in the hurdles and high
jump because he could use all
his parkour skills.

The loudspeaker crackled and we
heard the principal's voice boom
over the system.

"It's now time for tag!" he announced.

The crowd cheered. We **LOVED** tag. Everyone got to attach tags to their waist. Then we were put into teams. The aim was to chase one another and pull off the tags from the other teams. The team who stole the most tags was the winner.

Zeke, Jez, and I high-fived when we were all put on the same team—the purple team.

"Are you ready to get **BLOXXED?"** a teasing voice said.

Trip and his blockhead friends, Elle and Levi, were on the orange team.

"We're gonna **SMASH** you!" Trip goaded.

"He thinks he's the biggest pro," Jez said, rolling her eyes on her wide face.

We attached our tags and took our places.

"Ready? **GO!**"

We all started running around, dodging the enemy as well as chasing them down for their tags. Zeke was a **TOTAL PRO.** He could do backflips and cool somersaults, which confused the other team. By the end of the first couple of minutes, he'd captured five tags, including Elle's and Levi's. But

Trip was still running around, stealing everyone's tags.

"We've gotta get Trip," Jez panted. "He's the best on their side."

Zeke and I nodded.

"I'll get him to chase me, and then, Zeke, you come up behind him and take his tag," I said.

"On it!" Zeke yelled as he ran off in the opposite direction.

I saw Trip chasing down another purple team member.

"Hey, blockhead!" I yelled in his direction. "You can't catch me!"

Trip looked up and snarled, "I'm gonna get you, Ari Avatar!"

He started to chase me, but I ducked and weaved through the other players. He wasn't interested in any other tags— he just wanted to get me. I waved a signal to Zeke to start planning his attack on Trip.

But Trip was gaining on me. I had to move fast or he was going to steal my tag.

"Zeke, help!" I panted tiredly. I could feel Trip's breath on my neck as he reached out to grab my tag.

But then a **DEAFENING** noise sounded from above.

"ROOOOOOAAAAARRRR!"

Everyone looked up and screamed as a huge shadow was cast over the sports field.

"What on earth . . .?"

There was a ginormous **RED DRAGON** flying overhead.

It was Ember!

Ember **BELLOWED** with a grimace. His eyes locked on Trip, then he scrunched up his face and let out a **SPOUT OF FIRE** from his nostrils.

Everyone screamed and ran
for cover.

"Ari! It's Ember! I think he thinks
Trip is trying to hurt you!" Jez
said breathlessly. "He doesn't
realize this is just a game!"

"Ember, no!" I yelled. "We're playing
a **GAME!**"

But Ember didn't pay any
attention. He swooped down on
Trip, trying to blast him with his
fire breath.

Trip screamed and ran, but Ember

was too fast. He kept swooping.

"Ember, **STOP!**" I yelled.

Ember took one big diving swoop and reached out his front claws. He grabbed Trip by the shoulders and picked him up into the air.

Trip **SQUEALED.**

Ember flew around the sky, doing loops and twists. Trip continued to scream in terror.

"What are you gonna do?!" Zeke gasped.

"Yeah—he might hurt Trip if he thinks he's an enemy. I mean, Trip is a **TOTAL NOOB,** but he doesn't deserve to be thrown in the ocean or burned to a crisp," Jez said.

Jez was right. I looked around the oval for something to attract Ember.

"There!" I shouted.

My friends nodded, understanding my idea. We ran as fast as we could to the food stalls. Next to the snow cone stand was a big **POPCORN MACHINE!**

The avatar serving the popcorn was hiding underneath it.

"Can we borrow your stand?" Zeke said.

The avatar whimpered and nodded.

The popcorn machine was on wheels, with handles on the other side, just like a wheelbarrow. But it was big and heavy. Zeke, Jez, and I began to push. It took all our combined strength to lever the handle upward so it was balancing on the wheels. We rolled it across the grass, calling for

Ember to look down. But Ember was too distracted, flying through the air with a terrified Trip in his grip.

Ember suddenly turned and started to fly away from the field.

"EMBER, COME BACK!"

I screamed. Who knew where he was planning to take Trip?!

"There!" Jez was pointing at the school marching band.

I nodded and ran over, grabbing the tuba from one of the petrified students. Taking a big breath, I blew.

POOOOOM!

Ember hesitated
in the air.

POOOOOM!

He turned to find the source of
the noise. I ran ahead.

POOOOOM!

Ember saw me with the tuba but
wasn't interested. I ran over to
the popcorn machine and blew the
tuba again.

POOOOOOM!

I climbed on top of the popcorn machine, but Ember wasn't looking at me at all. How was I going to get his attention?

Suddenly, out of nowhere, I heard a familiar high-pitched yapping. It was **CODA!** She was tearing across the grass toward me, with her tongue hanging out of her mouth. She took a massive leap into the air and landed next to me on top of the popcorn machine.

"Whoa, **PARKOUR DOG!**" someone yelled, pointing as Coda somersaulted through the air.

Ember couldn't miss the flying dog and he looked straight down at us. That's when he saw what we were standing on. His eyes lit up. He put Trip down on the top of a tall tree and swooped over to the machine.

"Come on, boy!" I yelled. "Lots of yummy popcorn!"

"YAP, YAP, YAP!" barked Coda.

Ember hovered above the machine

and then landed on top of it next to Coda. The machine only had a few buckets of popcorn left in it, which Ember inhaled quickly. He looked inside the glass case, searching for more.

"Sorry, all gone, boy," I said, shrugging.

But Ember didn't think so. Hanging off the side of the cart were several huge bags of **UNPOPPED KERNELS.**

"Um, Ember . . ." I warned.

But before I could say anything

more, a **STREAM OF FIRE** burst out of his nose. The bags of popcorn kernels let off a giant bang and popcorn spilled out all over the oval, covering the grass. Lots of avatars cheered and started eating it off the ground.

Some made snow angels in the popcorn. Others chucked it up into the air.

Seconds later, Dad appeared. He was all puffed out from running to catch up with Coda. He had a chain in his hand and he quickly ran toward us and threw it over for me to place it back on Ember's collar.

"How'd he get out?" I said breathlessly as we all jumped down to the ground.

"He snapped the chain right off.

It was **CODA** who alerted me,"
Dad said, giving Coda a pat. But
then Dad looked back up at Ember.
"Ari, he's grown so much just since
this morning!"

Dad was right. How big would he
be tomorrow?

"Ari, I think you know we can't
keep Ember," Dad said quietly.

I didn't want to hear that, but
I knew it was true.

"We'll find you a good home,"
I promised Ember.

He nuzzled into me and I hugged
him tightly.

Meanwhile, Trip could be heard
screaming from the top of the
tree, "GET ME DOOOOOOOWN!"

ONE WEEK LATER

After the episode at school, it was pretty obvious we couldn't keep a dragon. We did some research and it turned out there was a

DRAGON SANCTUARY

a couple of hours away from Blockville. They kept the dragons in a big, open area, and they were free to fly around and play with their own kind. The owner of the sanctuary said we could come anytime we liked, and Mom had promised I could visit Ember today.

As I got ready to go out the door, Mom stopped me. "I'm sorry it didn't work out with Ember," she said. "Do you think you'd like to try a different pet?"

I thought for a moment. Then I called out, **"CODA!"**

Coda came bounding down the stairs carrying her own leash and a ball.

"Nah," I said. "I didn't realize it, but I had my **DREAM PET** here all along."

Coda jumped
up and licked
my face.
"Ready to go
see Ember,

Coda? Then we'll go to the park!"

Coda yapped and jumped on her
hind legs.

I guess she wasn't the rarest pet
in the world, but I didn't care. She
was my dream pet, after all.